NORWICH J 791.45 RAVE D
Dougherty, Terri.
Raven-Symoné

NOV 17 2009

GUERNSEY MEMORIAL LIBRARY

0 00 04 0238916 7

Guernsey Memorial Library
3 Court Street, Norwich, NY 13815
(607) 334-4034
www.guernseylibrary.org

MODERN ROLE MODELS

Raven-Symoné

Terri Dougherty

Mason Crest Publishers

Produced by OTTN Publishing in association with
21st Century Publishing and Communications, Inc.

Copyright © 2009 by Mason Crest Publishers. All rights reserved. No part of this publication may be reproduced or transmitted in any form or by any means, electronic or mechanical, including photocopying, recording, taping, or any information storage and retrieval system, without permission from the publisher.

MASON CREST PUBLISHERS INC.
370 Reed Road
Broomall, Pennsylvania 19008
(866) MCP-BOOK (toll free)
www.masoncrest.com

Printed in the United States of America.

First Printing

9 8 7 6 5 4 3 2 1

Library of Congress Cataloging-in-Publication Data

Dougherty, Terri.
　Raven-Symoné / Terri Dougherty.
　　p. cm. — (Modern role models)
ISBN-13: 978-1-4222-0508-2 (hardcover) — ISBN-13: 978-1-4222-0795-6 (pbk.)
 1. Raven, 1985–　—Juvenile literature. 2. African American singers—Biography—Juvenile literature. 3. Television actors and actresses—United States—Biography—Juvenile literature. 4. African American actors—Biography—Juvenile literature. I. Title.
ML3930.R28D68 2008
791.4502'8092—dc22
[B]　　　　　　　　　　　　　　　　　　　　　　　　　　　2008020403

Publisher's note:
All quotations in this book come from original sources, and contain the spelling and grammatical inconsistencies of the original text.

CROSS-CURRENTS

In the ebb and flow of the currents of life we are each influenced by many people, places, and events that we directly experience or have learned about. Throughout the chapters of this book you will come across **CROSS-CURRENTS** reference boxes. These boxes direct you to a **CROSS-CURRENTS** section in the back of the book that contains fascinating and informative sidebars and related pictures. Go on. ▶▶

CONTENTS

1 Cute Kid, Generous Actress   5

2 The Road to Stardom   11

3 She's So Raven   19

4 New Challenges   29

5 Beyond Raven   39

Cross-Currents   48

Chronology   56

Accomplishments & Awards   57

Further Reading & Internet Resources   59

Glossary   60

Notes   61

Index   63

Picture Credits   64

About the Author   64

Raven-Symoné shows off one of the awards that she won at the 38th annual NAACP Image Awards. She received the awards at a ceremony in Los Angeles on March 2, 2007. After more than 18 years as a television star, Raven-Symoné has established herself as one of the leading comic actors of her generation.

Cute Kid, Generous Actress

WHEN THE STARS CAME OUT FOR THE 2007 NAACP Image Awards, actress Raven-Symoné was among them. She won an award for Outstanding Performance in a Youth/Children's Series/Special. Her show *That's So Raven* was named Outstanding Children's Program. The young actress was honored for more than her talent. She was also recognized for promoting a positive image.

At the same event she presented an award to the man who had given her a start in television. Bill Cosby was inducted into the Image Awards Hall of Fame. Nearly 20 years earlier, Cosby had chosen Raven-Symoné to be a regular on his hit TV **series** *The Cosby Show*. When she started working with him in 1989, Raven-Symoné was only three years old. Young as she was, she won the respect of her **costars** and the admiration of viewers.

> **CROSS-CURRENTS**
> *Bill Cosby, who gave Raven-Symoné her start in television, is a highly respected performer. To learn more, read "Bill Cosby." Go to page 48.* ▸▸

RAVEN-SYMONÉ

➤ Growing Up on TV ⬅

Raven-Symoné has grown up as an actress. She kept acting in television shows even after *The Cosby Show* ended in 1992. She played a character on the series *Hangin' with Mr. Cooper* and then, in 2003, she got her own series on the Disney Channel. *That's So Raven* sent the 17-year-old star to a new level of fame.

Raven-Symoné's knack for comedy has made her one the most popular young actresses today. On *Raven*, she became known for taking **pratfalls** and making crazy faces. She knows how to say her lines and **mug** for the camera, and no matter what she is working on she can make people laugh. **Producer** Ron Trippe, who worked with her on the **animated film** *Everyone's Hero*, called her:

> "A very talented young actress that everyone in the business should have a chance to work with."

Thanks to **reruns** of *Cosby*, *Cooper*, and *Raven*, kids can watch her on all three shows. She also appears in movies and on the Internet with her own Web site. No matter what she is doing, Raven-Symoné is always entertaining.

➤ Earning Respect ⬅

Raven-Symoné is respected for more than just her acting talent. Using her fame, she has begun building a business empire. She started a clothing line and had a fragrance named after her. There are *That's So Raven* books, DVDs, games, and bedsheets. More than $400 million of these *Raven*-themed products have been sold.

In 2008, *US Magazine* called Raven-Symoné one of the 10 Most Powerful Girls. Her power comes from her earnings as well as her influence.

As she outgrew the Raven Baxter character, Raven-Symoné looked for other ways to expand her career. She has made movies and shared the hobbies that interested her. Raven-Symoné loves crafts and cooking, and hopes one day to have her own show that features cooking and craft segments. She is always full of ideas, and shares them on her Web site.

➤ Role Model ⬅

Raven-Symoné is also admired for what she does, and does not do, when she is not on screen. Raven-Symoné helps others and

Cute Kid, Generous Actress

A story about Raven-Symoné in the March 2007 issue of *Ebony* magazine called her "the $400 million woman." Over the past few years, sales of bookbags, clothing, dolls, and other items featuring Raven's name or picture have exceeded that amount. Her share of these sales have made Raven-Symoné one of the wealthiest young people in America.

RAVEN-SYMONÉ

Raven-Symoné (center) smiles as she displays the 2007 North Star Award, presented by the National Association for Multi-ethnicity in Communications (NAMIC). The award honors an individual for exceptional efforts to reflect diversity in programming. Rondell Sheridan (left), her *That's So Raven* costar, presented the award, along with actress Niecy Nash (right).

contributes to charities. She does not go to parties or try to grab attention from photographers.

One of Raven-Symoné's favorite charities is the Make-A-Wish Foundation. She helps bring joy to children who are terminally ill by granting their wishes to experience something special.

The young actress also promotes the National Safe Kids Campaign, which encourages home safety. She raises money for the Children's

Miracle Network, a charity that helps children's hospitals. Another charity Raven works with is Girls Incorporated. It encourages girls to be strong and believe in themselves. It offers educational programs and promotes positive values. Its mission fits right in with what Raven wants to do with her life. She comments,

> "I'm focusing on girl power—girls are beautiful no matter their size, hair color, skin color. Beauty doesn't mean being like everyone else. It's owning who you are and feeling good about it."

BEING HERSELF

Raven-Symoné has received awards for the way she lives her life. In addition to the NAACP Image Award she received in 2007, she also won Image Awards for her work on *That's So Raven* in 2004, 2005, 2006, and 2008. She was nominated for Image Awards in 2002 for *Dr. Dolittle 2*, and in 1996 for *Hangin' with Mr. Cooper*.

Raven-Symoné does not structure her life around winning awards, however. She lives her life trying to stay true to herself. She does not try to attract notice by going to parties or events. She stays away from alcohol and drugs. She likes staying home, doing crafts, and being herself. She is so focused on her career and charity work that she has had no problem staying out of trouble.

Raven-Symoné does not worry about trying to be super thin or dressing up in public. She is a young woman who is proud of who she is and how she looks and says she is not about to change:

> "Being beautiful is not being like everybody else. I think it's messed up that little girls only see one type of person. It gives them a false image of who we all really are. Girls come up to me and say, 'I'm not like everyone on TV, and finally we can look up to someone who's larger than a size 2.' I'm not a pinkie-thin blond thing, and I never will be. I'm me."

CROSS-CURRENTS

During her career, Raven-Symoné has won five Image Awards. To learn more about this honor, read "The NAACP Image Awards." Go to page 49.

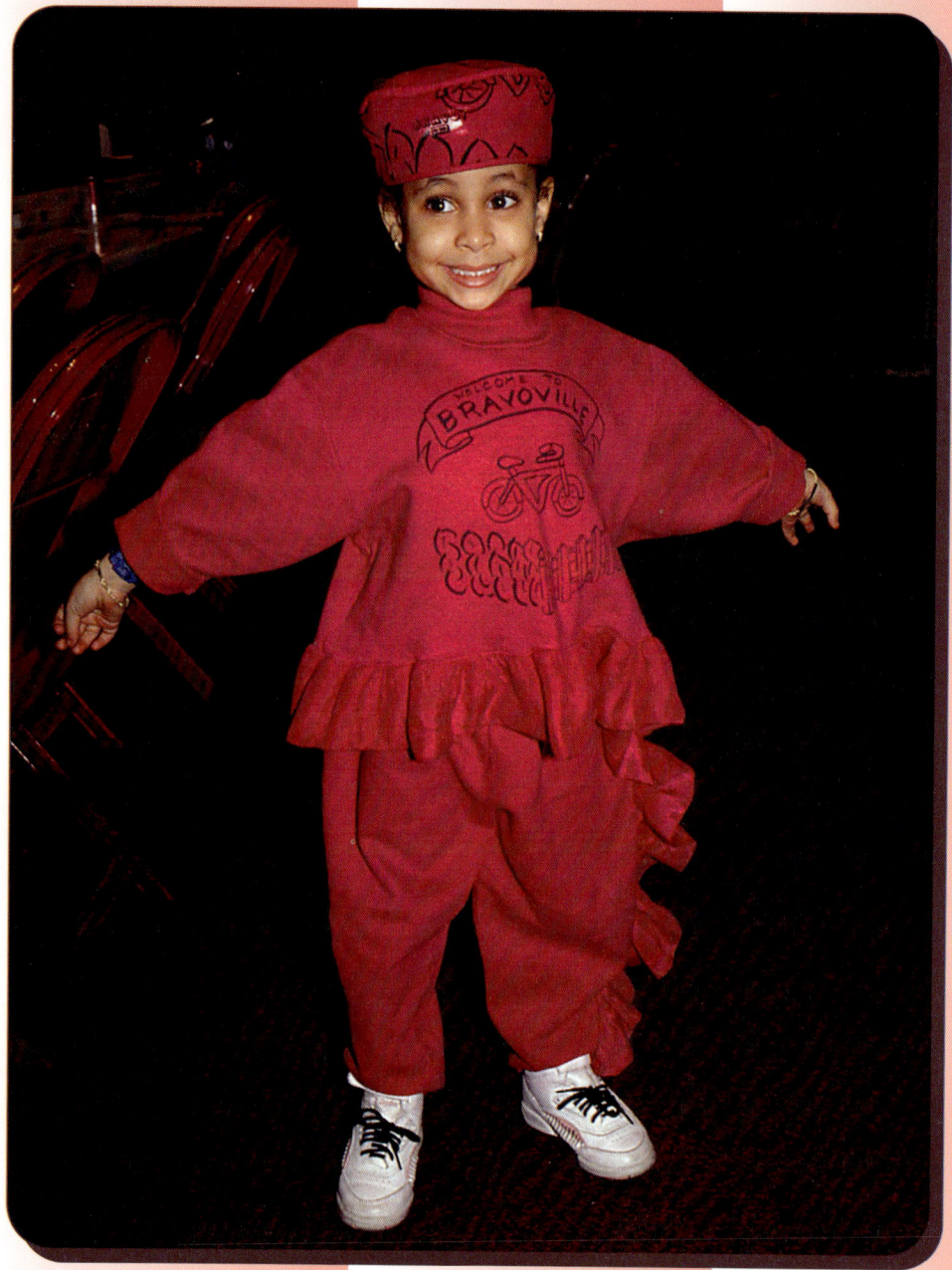

From a young age, Raven-Symoné has been in the public eye. She first came to national attention when she was just three years old. She was selected for a part on the groundbreaking NBC series *The Cosby Show*. When that series ended, Raven-Symoné went on to work on other television programs.

2

The Road to Stardom

RAVEN-SYMONÉ CHRISTINA PEARMAN WAS BORN December 10, 1985, in Atlanta, Georgia. Her parents are Christopher Pearman and Lydia Gaulden Pearman. She has a younger brother named Blaize. Her father became her manager when she began her career and continues to help manage her affairs. Her mother worked in computer science before Raven-Symoné began acting. She also helps manage her daughter's career.

Young Star

Raven-Symoné began modeling when she was 16 months old. She could be seen in newspaper and magazine ads in the Atlanta area. At age two Raven-Symoné signed with the Ford Modeling agency, one of the best-known modeling agencies in the world. The family traveled to New York so Raven-Symoné could go to **auditions**. In addition to appearing in ads in newspapers and magazines, the toddler also began doing commercials.

RAVEN-SYMONÉ

An outgoing little girl, Raven-Symoné also showed an interest in acting when she was very young. When she first saw *The Cosby Show* on television at the age of three, she wanted to be part of it. She insisted that she could do what the kids on the show were doing.

Raven-Symoné got to meet the creator of the show, Bill Cosby, when she auditioned for his movie *Ghost Dad*. She was too young for that movie, but Cosby was taken by the little girl. He told her that if she could memorize three pages of a script, he would put her on his show. Raven-Symoné memorized eight pages, and Cosby kept his word. She became part of his series *The Cosby Show*. In 1989, Raven-Symoné began playing Olivia, the stepchild of Cosby's character's daughter Denise.

> **CROSS-CURRENTS**
> In its day, The Cosby Show was the most popular program on television. For more details, read "The Cosby Show." Go to page 50.

In her first acting job, Raven-Symoné stepped right into the spotlight. She was not just part of the background, but had scenes with Cosby and the other stars. She provided humor by putting adults like Cosby in uncomfortable situations. In one **episode**, she talked about where babies come from. In another, she asked about Santa Claus's race. By the end of the first season, the audience was so taken with her that *TV Guide* magazine wrote a profile about the little girl. At age four and a half, she was featured in *TV Guide* as "Cosby's Rockin' Raven."

Working with Cosby helped her learn about comic timing, Raven-Symoné has said. But being on the show hardly seemed like work. Mostly, she just enjoyed herself. The show brought the young actress her first awards. In 1991, she received the Young Artist Award for Exceptional Performance by a Young Actress Under Nine. She was also nominated for a Young Artist Award in 1990 and 1993.

⇒ SINGING CAREER ⇐

Acting was not the only thing Raven-Symoné wanted to do. She wanted to sing, too. After *The Cosby Show* ended in 1992, her father tried to interest record companies in signing her to a **contract**. She became the youngest artist ever to sign with MCA records and recorded a song written by Missy Elliot, "That's What Little Girls Are Made Of." The song was released in 1993 and the single was on the album *Here's to New Dreams*.

The Road to Stardom

Wearing a yellow ribbon in her hair, Raven-Symoné is pictured at the center of the family in this scene from *The Cosby Show*. After being added to the cast in 1989, Raven often drew laughs by asking the adult characters tough questions. During Raven's three years on *Cosby*, it was one of the most popular programs on television.

She showed off her singing talent in other ways as well. In 1990, she performed the song "Rainbow Connection" on the television show *The Muppets at Walt Disney World*. She also sang with the Boys Choir of Harlem for that group's 25th anniversary celebration.

⇒ Busy Actress ⇐

Raven-Symoné did not leave acting behind after *Cosby* ended. She continued her career and was soon splitting her time between the family's home in her native Atlanta and Los Angeles. In Los Angeles, she went to auditions and landed several small television **roles**. In 1992, she appeared on *The Fresh Prince of Bel-Air*, a television series

RAVEN-SYMONÉ

starring Will Smith. She got a small role in the television miniseries *Queen* in 1993, and a role as a singer in the television mystery movie *Blindsided*. In 1994, she appeared in her first movie, *The Little Rascals*.

The year before *Rascals* was released, Raven-Symoné nabbed her next steady job. She became a regular on the series *Hangin' with Mr. Cooper*. The **sitcom** starred Mark Curry as a teacher and basketball coach living with a friend, his cousin, and his cousin's daughter. Raven-Symoné played Nicole, the daughter, an inquisitive child. In 1994, she was nominated as the Best Youth Comedienne for her work on the show.

The success of *The Cosby Show*, about an affluent African-American family, helped to make possible other television programs about black families. One of these was *Hangin' with Mr. Cooper*, which aired on ABC from 1992 to 1997. Raven-Symoné (pictured at left, in a scene from *Hangin' with Mr. Cooper*) joined the cast in the second season.

The Road to Stardom

Hangin' with Mr. Cooper ended its run in 1997. Raven-Symoné was soon working again. In 1998, she was chosen for a significant role in a movie with Eddie Murphy. She played Murphy's daughter in *Dr. Dolittle.* Murphy was impressed by her performance. He said:

> **"Working with her and seeing her nail her lines was just amazing to me."**

Raven-Symoné felt fortunate to be able to play characters with a range of personalities. She usually was cast as someone's daughter, but each character had its own personality. She described her character on *Hangin' with Mr. Cooper* as a country girl, while Charisse in *Dr. Dolittle* had a sassier personality. She said she was fortunate not to be **typecast** into one style of role.

Down Side

Although she was working regularly, Raven-Symoné did not get every role she tried out for. When she was rejected for a part, she did not take it personally. She just kept auditioning for the roles she wanted to play. She said:

> **"I've gotten rejected so many times that I probably shouldn't be in the business. But it gave me thick skin and I just keep on pushing, slowly and surely."**

When she was not acting, Raven-Symoné returned home to school in Atlanta. It was not easy to head back to school at first. She did not receive a warm welcome. In an effort to ease the transition, the principal had warned students not to ask for her autograph. Unfortunately, some of the students thought Raven-Symoné had asked for this and labeled her as a snob.

> **"I get there and there'd be people eyeing me before they even knew me. So I would stick to myself. I wasn't that popular."**

Eventually, she made some friends and they enjoyed going to football games and pep rallies. But even then she still considered herself an outcast. She was never one of the popular students.

RAVEN-SYMONÉ

As a teenager, Raven-Symoné kept busy. She sometimes found it difficult to complete her schoolwork because of her film and television roles. Although Raven-Symoné felt that she was not part of the popular crowd at her school in Atlanta, she earned good grades in school and had many friends.

The Road to Stardom

🟠 Back to Work 🟠

Raven-Symoné was not always able to go to class, however. Her acting work took her away from home and school. She still had to keep up with her schoolwork. Her assignments were mailed to her when she had to miss school because she was making a movie or television show.

Raven-Symoné was not a huge star but worked regularly. Between 1999 and 2001, she had roles in the movie *Zenon: Girl of the 21st Century*, *Happily Ever After: Fairy Tales for Every Child*, and a **sequel** to *Dr. Dolittle*. She also appeared in two episodes of the television series *My Wife and Kids* and did voice work on an episode of *The Proud Family*.

Although Raven-Symoné was barely a teen, she was already a role model for other kids. By 1998 she had become involved in the Safe Kids home safety campaign and D.A.R.E., Drug Abuse Resistance Education.

While she continued to act, Raven-Symoné did not abandon her singing career. She released the album *Undeniable* in 1999, and toured as an opening act for 'N Sync. While she had a strong voice, her singing career couldn't match her talent for acting. Although acting meant she had to deal with rejection and jealous looks at school, she was happy it was part of her life.

> ❝People always ask me if my childhood was hard. I say 'No, this is my childhood, and I'm having a great time. . . . Everything that I do is fun. My parents try to get work for me that I will learn from and have fun while doing.'❞

Raven-Symoné got her big break in 2002, when she was chosen to play the leading role in a new Disney Channel series. The show, originally called *Absolutely Psychic*, was soon renamed for her: *That's So Raven*. The success of *That's So Raven* launched Raven-Symoné to a new level of fame.

3

She's So Raven

IN 2002 RAVEN-SYMONÉ TRIED OUT FOR A ROLE IN a show called *Absolutely Psychic.* She auditioned for a supporting role. The show's executives were so impressed with her performance, they decided to make her the star of the show. They also renamed the show. It became *That's So Raven* and it put the 17-year-old actress in the spotlight.

That's So Raven premiered on the Disney Channel on January 17, 2003. In addition to Raven-Symoné, the show starred Rondell Sheridan and T'Keyah Crystal Kemiah as Raven's parents, Kyle Massey as her younger brother Kyle, and Orlando Brown and Anneliese van der Poi as her best friends. It quickly became a hit, particularly among young viewers.

During the first years of the show's run, Raven-Symoné decided to rename herself. She now wanted to be known only as Raven.

With the *That's So Raven* role, Raven had the chance to show what she could do with her own style of comedy. She played Raven

RAVEN-SYMONÉ

Baxter, a high school student who could see into the future. Her character wanted things to work out for those around her. When her glimpses into the future showed something bad happening, she would try to straighten things out, and she'd often get herself into a sticky situation in the process.

The show's scenes usually involved outrageous situations and slapstick humor. For example, when Raven had a vision of her younger brother telling her he hated her, she tried to throw him a great birthday party. She was determined to stop the vision from coming true so she hired an animal trainer to perform. When the trainer got sick, she had to wrestle an anaconda to satisfy the party guests. When the snake turned out to be fake, the party fell apart. Raven's shows always had a warm ending, however, and things ended up working out between Raven and her brother.

The show allowed Raven to transform into other characters using makeup and elaborate costumes. In one episode she dressed up as a plumber. In another she played three of Raven Baxter's relatives, including a baby and an old woman. She had to spend hours in the makeup chair to transform into these other characters. Raven loved the opportunity it gave her to learn something new, however. She liked the challenge of having to remember how each separate character was supposed to react in a situation:

> "It showed me that I love to do this kind of work."

ATTRACTING ATTENTION

Raven's starring role brought recognition to the young actress. Her show was funny and had stories that kids and teens could relate to. *That's So Raven* became one of the most-watched programs on the Disney Channel and aired in 100 different countries. She earned a Teen Choice Award, a Kids' Choice Award, and a Black Reel Award for her role in the show.

Raven did other work for the Disney Channel as well. In 2002 she began working on the Disney animated series *Kim Possible*. The series was about a high school teen who was a superhero. Christy Carlson Romano provided the voice of Kim, while Raven gave voice to Kim's friend Monique.

Raven continued to voice the character through 2007. She was better known for her live-action television show, but she earned

She's So Raven

Some of the stars of *That's So Raven*: (from left) T'Keyah Crystal Kemiah, who played Tanya Baxter, Raven's mother; Kyle Massey, who played Cory, Raven's younger brother; Raven-Symoné; and Rondell Sheridan, who played Raven's father, Victor Baxter. Other actors who starred in the show included Orlando Brown and Anneliese van der Poi, who played Raven's best friends.

recognition for her voice work as well. In 2005, she was nominated for a BET Comedy Award for her work on *Kim Possible*.

Cheetah Girl

Although she was already the star of a television show and doing voice work for a cartoon, Raven saw another project she was interested in. When she heard about a movie called *The Cheetah Girls*, she approached Disney Channel executives. She let them know it was something she would like to do. They felt she would be perfect for a role in the movie. Producer Debra Martin Chase saw something special in Raven. She noted:

> **She has that intangible thing—the It factor people always talk about.**

The 2003 movie told the story of four girls who form a pop band. They all come from different backgrounds, but music brings them together. As they try to reach their goal of becoming singing stars, their different attitudes almost break the group apart. However, their love for music and support of each other eventually wins out. In addition to Raven as Galleria, the show also featured Adrienne Bailon as Chanel, Kiely Williams as Aqua, and Sabrina Bryan as Dorinda.

The movie lacked the physical comedy of *Raven* and had more dramatic moments. This allowed Raven to expand her acting range and show off her singing talent. Both the opportunity to sing and the movie's message attracted the teen to the project. She said:

> **I love *The Cheetah Girls* because it's very multicultural. And it's filled with morals, but it doesn't preach to the audience. Also, I got to sing and dance and hang out with my girls. We had a wonderful time.**

The Cheetah Girls was a huge hit. When it aired in 2003, it set a record with 6.5 million viewers. When the show was released on DVD, almost a million copies were sold.

Girls liked the show because they could identify with its characters, Raven said. The characters worked through tough times to reach

She's So Raven

Raven-Symoné (second from left) with her *Cheetah Girls* costars: Sabrina Bryan, Kiely Williams, and Adrienne Bailon. The 2003 movie was a huge Disney Channel hit. The Foundation for the Advancement of African Americans in Film nominated *The Cheetah Girls* for a Black Reel Award for Best Network/Cable Film. Raven-Symoné was also nominated for a Black Reel, as Best Actress-Television Movie/Mini-Series.

their goal of performing. This was a dream many young girls could identify with. In addition, the characters' different backgrounds helped the show reach a broad audience. That's what Raven liked about the show:

> ❝ The cast is so diverse that every girl can relate to at least one of the characters. Plus, a lot of young girls want to be stars, whether it's singing or acting, and they get to watch these girls struggle to make their dreams come true and overcome obstacles. ❞

RAVEN-SYMONÉ

Making Music

The Cheetah Girls gave Raven the opportunity to return to her interest in singing. It was a successful move. The **soundtrack** from *The Cheetah Girls* sold two million copies.

The other members of *The Cheetah Girls* cast went on tour, but Raven did not appear with the group. Instead, Raven followed *The Cheetah Girls* album with a solo effort. She released *This Is My Time*

Raven-Symoné (second from right) was among nine young ladies pictured on the cover when *Vanity Fair* magazine focused on teenage stars in its July 2003 issue. Others on the cover included (from left) Amanda Bynes, Ashley and Mary-Kate Olsen, Mandy Moore, Hilary Duff, Alexis Bledel, Evan Rachel Wood, and Lindsay Lohan.

in 2004, which featured the single "Backflip." Her goal was to create an album with a distinct sound that appealed to a broad age range:

> **"I want people to hear a new sound. I'm trying to mix the deep R&B sound with fun track beats, and really alternative rock lyrics."**

The title of the album reflected her desire to pursue a singing career for a little while. She loved both music and acting, but did not have the time to focus on both at once. Because acting gave her the chance to do something new every week, she chose that route most of the time. However, she still loved music.

The album was a personal one for Raven. She cowrote five of the songs. Music allowed the young star to show more of her personality. When she sang or wrote music, she could be herself rather than a character.

Raven delivered positive messages on the album. The song "Mystify" talked about capturing someone's attention without wearing revealing clothing. In "Life Is Beautiful," she talked about how life could be appreciated without focusing on material things.

The singer wanted *This Is My Time* to appeal to everyone in the family. She mixed soul with hip-hop and brought in a variety of musical styles. Its hallmark was its upbeat message, however. The CD featured clean lyrics and delivered a message of self-respect.

The CD was a step forward in Raven's musical career but was not a big seller. It sold around 235,000 copies, which was tiny compared to the millions sold by *The Cheetah Girls* CD. However, it did give Raven the opportunity to follow her interest in singing.

Fit for a Princess

Raven returned to acting with an appearance in the 2004 Disney movie *The Princess Diaries 2: Royal Engagement*. The sequel to *The Princess Diaries* starred Anne Hathaway as Mia Thermopolis, a young lady who is struggling to learn the ropes of royalty. Veteran singer and actress Julie Andrews played Mia's grandmother, Queen Clarisse Renaldi, and Raven played Mia's friend Asana.

Raven's acting role in the movie was not a large one, but the film also gave her the chance to do some singing. Her song "This Is My Time" was part of the movie's soundtrack, and she also got to

RAVEN-SYMONÉ

"Raven Baxter is so excited and happy and kind of crazy, and I'm not that way," Raven-Symoné explained in an interview, when asked about the differences between her and her character. "I kind of stay to myself. The ways we're similar? We both love fashion. But I'll wear sweats to anything if I'm allowed to."

sing a duet with Andrews. Andrews is an Oscar-winning actress who has impressed audiences in musicals such as *Mary Poppins* and *The Sound of Music*. Performing a duet with such an accomplished singer was a thrill for Raven. As a child, she had watched *Mary Poppins* so many times that her mother had to buy a new tape. She told an interviewer:

> **"I got to sing with Mary Poppins [Julie Andrews], and lemme tell you it was the best day! Meeting her was a dream!"**

Raven also contributed a song to the soundtrack for the 2004 movie *Ella Enchanted*. Her song "True to Your Heart" was featured in the film.

TRUE TO HERSELF

Staying true to herself remained Raven's goal. She never pretended to be someone she was not. When she arrived for a photo shoot for the magazine *Girl's Life* in 2004, she was not wearing designer clothes or makeup. She arrived in pink sweats and flip-flops.

She also showed her imperfections on the cover of her CD. The photo for *This Is My Time* showed pimples and pores on her skin. Raven did not bother to worry about what other people thought. She was too busy being herself. She wanted girls to realize that it was OK for them to be themselves.

She readily admits that she is a lot like other kids—she gets star-struck just like they do. When she met singer Janet Jackson, she was so awed that she could not think of anything to say. She recalled:

> **"I met Janet Jackson, and she probably thinks I'm a mute. I just stared and blinked, going 'uh, um. . . .' So sad. But it was Janet people! I'm a girl just like you!"**

CROSS-CURRENTS

If you'd like to find out why Raven-Symoné felt honored to work on *Princess Diaries* with Julie Andrews, read "Julie Andrews." Go to page 50.

CROSS-CURRENTS

Insights into Raven-Symoné's popularity with young audiences and her knack for comic acting can be found in "Raven's Secret." Go to page 52.

This photo of Raven-Symoné appeared on a promotional poster for *That's So Raven*. After three seasons had been completed, Raven-Symoné had an opportunity to take over the show's production. This gave Raven more control over the way each show turned out. To help with the task, she formed a new company, That's So Productions.

New Challenges

BY THE TIME SHE WAS 20 YEARS OLD, RAVEN WAS an experienced actress. She had starred in a successful television show, appeared in popular movies, and pursued a singing career. The young star was not one to dwell on what she had accomplished, however. She wanted to challenge herself by tackling new goals.

One change in Raven's life occurred in 2004, when she changed her name back to Raven-Symoné. She had originally changed her name to make signing autographs easier and to be more similar to her television character, Raven Baxter. However, she admitted to reporters that she had missed using her full name.

That's So Raven remained one of the Disney Channel's most popular shows. In 2005, it was nominated for a prime-time Emmy award. The show was so popular that Disney decided to break a longstanding corporate rule. The company had always limited its shows to 65 episodes, feeling that a series began to get stale at that point. *That's So Raven* was the first Disney show to have its contract extended beyond that point. Ultimately, 100 episodes of *That's So Raven* would be aired.

Raven enjoyed playing her character, and continued to do it well, but she also wanted to do something more. She looked behind the scenes for a new challenge. In the 2006 season, Raven became the producer of several episodes of *That's So Raven*. This new title meant that Raven was in charge of more than just reciting her lines and acting her part. She was more involved in creating each episode of the show, and had to make sure things went smoothly as the episodes came together.

More Production

The television show *That's So Raven* was not the only place where Raven-Symoné's influence was felt. She also provided input for the **music videos** that were shot for a soundtrack from the show. The CD *That's So Raven Too* featured several songs by Raven-Symoné. It also included tracks by other stars from the show, as well as young singers like Aly & AJ and Jesse McCartney.

Raven-Symoné's experience showed. She had a vision for the music videos and she was able to translate that vision to others. Damon Whiteside, the vice president of marketing for Disney Records, commented that Raven-Symoné succeeded as a producer because she knew the entertainment business so well:

> **"She's so on the mark and so talented because she's grown up in it. She has a very strong sense of who she is, and who she wants to be, and where she's going."**

More Cheetah

Raven-Symoné was also a producer of the sequel to the popular Cheetah Girls movie, *The Cheetah Girls 2*. This 2006 movie reunited the original cast and took the girls to Spain. In Barcelona, they competed in a contest for new singing groups. The Cheetah Girls realized that they had very different interests, and for a time they considered breaking up. In the end, however, they found strength in being together.

The high-energy movie was filled with music and dance numbers. As with *The Cheetah Girls*, it was a hit with young girls. The CD from the movie soundtrack included several tracks by Raven-Symoné.

New Challenges

The Cheetah Girls were very popular, but Raven-Symoné still had an acting career to be concerned with. She did not record the next CD, *Cheetah Girls TCG*, with the other three Cheetahs or tour with them. She pursued her solo singing career and acting jobs instead.

> **CROSS-CURRENTS**
> "Who's Who in The Cheetah Girls" provides background on the four main characters from the hit film. Go to page 53.

✹ VOICE WORK ✺

In addition to producing *Cheetah Girls 2*, Raven-Symoné continued to work behind the scenes in other ways. One was by lending her voice to animated characters. She had been providing the voice of

Raven-Symoné has provide the voice for Monique, a supporting character on the Disney Channel cartoon *Kim Possible*. (Monique, who is one of Kim's best friends, is standing next to the car, wearing the red dress, in this picture of the *Kim Possible* characters.) Original episodes of the show aired on the Disney Channel from 2002 to 2007.

RAVEN-SYMONÉ

Monique on the animated series *Kim Possible* for several years, and in 2004 she had a small role as the voice of Danielle in the movie *Fat Albert*. This movie reunited her with Bill Cosby, who had created the television cartoon *Fat Albert* in the 1970s.

In 2006, Raven-Symoné took on another animated project. The movie *Everyone's Hero* was set in 1932 and told the story of a boy who travels across the country to return a lucky baseball bat to New York Yankees slugger Babe Ruth. Raven-Symoné provided the voice for Marti Brewster, the daughter of a Negro League star, who helped get the bat back to Ruth. The G-rated family movie stressed the message of never giving up.

☀ Turning to Drama ☀

Raven-Symoné was committed to offering movies and television shows that families could enjoy, but she did not want to limit herself to starring in comic roles. She turned to more serious fare in *For One Night*, a story about a Georgia girl who worked to integrate her high school's prom.

The movie, which premiered in 2006, focused on a more serious topic than her previous work, and Raven-Symoné was proud to be a part of it. However, it was not easy for her to switch gears from physical comedy. She put the same effort into this role that she did her television show, even when it was unpleasant for her. In one scene, she needed to cry. To put her in the right frame of mind the director told everyone on the set not to talk to her for a day. That did the trick, she said:

> **"By the end I was boo-hooing in front of the camera just because everyone was dissing me so badly. The director knew what he was doing."**

Based on a true story, *For One Night* tells about a high school that held two proms, one for black students and one for white. Raven-Symoné's character overcomes challenges as she works to bring the two groups together. The actress hoped that viewers would take the movie's theme to heart:

> **"I'm not going to change anybody's mind, but I wanted them to stop and think."**

New Challenges 33

In the 2006 film *For One Night*, Raven-Symoné played a high-school student who works to open her school's prom to both black and white students. The movie was based on the true story of Gerica McCrary, who in 2002 convinced students at her Georgia school to end a long tradition of holding separate proms for black and white students.

RAVEN-SYMONÉ

◈ MUSICAL MESSAGE ◈

Raven-Symoné also wanted to deliver a message through her music. She wanted to offer albums and a touring act that families could enjoy. She did not use lyrics or wear clothing that made parents or teens uncomfortable. In 2006 she released the album *From Then Until*. She went on tour that year, offering a family friendly show that was fine for her young fans as well as teens.

Raven-Symoné's commitment to family friendly music went beyond her own act. She also wanted the opening acts on tour to

In 2006, Raven-Symoné's album *From Then Until* was released by TMG Records. The album was actually a re-release of an earlier album, titled *Undeniable*, which had originally been recorded in 1999. It included songs Raven-Symoné had recorded when she was 13 years old, such as the single "With a Child's Heart."

New Challenges

share her point of view. She did not want her younger fans to be disappointed or surprised by what they saw. Some singers spiced up their shows with suggestive costumes and lyrics, but that was not Raven-Symoné's style. She and the groups on tour with her provided entertainment without shocking their fans. Raven-Symoné was comfortable with who she was and did not feel the need to try to attract attention by doing something outrageous.

Business Ventures

In some ways, Raven-Symoné is very different from the character she's played on television. She is not as zany or as much of a thrill-seeker as Raven Baxter. Raven-Symoné puts much more thought into her actions than her television counterpart.

Raven-Symoné did not mind being identified with her character, however. The show was a wholesome comedy that she was proud to be part of. In addition to filming episodes, she also promoted merchandise associated with the show.

Raven-Symoné's face appeared on a number of products, including sheets, lamps, a doll, and a Raven-themed Game Boy. DVDs of the show's episodes were also available. The venture was very profitable for both Disney and Raven-Symoné. Raven's merchandise was so successful that in early 2007 *Ebony* magazine called her the $400 million woman because of the money her name was bringing in. Executives did not see her popularity dimming any time soon. Rich Rose, president of Disney Channel Worldwide, said:

> "We see someone who is invaluable because of her appeal. She appeals to everyone—and that's rare. We have a partnership with her that is going to keep growing as long as she wants it."

Low Profile

Raven-Symoné was a wealthy teen with a popular show and a singing career. She did not flaunt her wealth or her position, however. Unlike some teen stars, Raven-Symoné rarely went to nightclubs. Her every move was not followed by a pack of photographers. She kept to herself and preferred to stay home when she was not working. She enjoyed putting on some sweatpants and relaxing, she said:

RAVEN-SYMONÉ

got milk?

Raven-Symoné has a good reputation because unlike some other young stars, she is not interested in wild parties. "I'm a homebody," she explained to *US magazine*. "I enjoy that a lot more than running the streets or going to clubs because I'm stimulating my mind and keeping it focused." Here, Raven poses for a "Got Milk?" ad.

New Challenges

> **"If you find me on one of my off days, I'm probably asleep at my house. I mind my own business, I kind of stay to myself."**

Raven-Symoné's desire to keep a low profile kept her off the covers of the gossip magazines that lined the supermarket shelves. This was both good and bad for the young actress. It gave her the ability to go out without worrying about being bothered, but also had the potential to dim her popularity. Some suspected she did not receive as much attention as some other stars because she was not thin and was African American. Raven-Symoné did not apologize for who she was, however:

> **"My fans know I love my cheese grits with shrimp, and I'm not giving them up to be a size 2. They know I wear a weave to make my hair look right and I don't always look glamorous all the time. I don't even worry about that type of stuff that much. You're not going to see me with clothes that just let everything hang out. And it's not because of my size, but because it's just not me."**

Raven-Symoné saw her career as a marathon rather than a sprint. She was not going to do too much and risk becoming overexposed. She wanted to pace herself for a long career.

Acting was far from the only thing the talented young star was interested in. She enjoyed singing and producing, and even thought about going to cooking school. She would rather be at a meeting than at a party, and had much more to think about than trying to come up with ways to get her photo onto the cover of magazines. There were ideas for her career she had not yet explored, and could not wait to try.

Since completing work on her television show, Raven-Symoné has worked on several different projects. In addition to making movies and releasing another album of her music, she has worked to develop a Web site. For her career as an entertainer to remain successful, Raven-Symoné will have to appeal to older people, as well as her current young fans.

5

Beyond Raven

IT CAN BE DIFFICULT FOR CHILD STARS TO EASE into roles for older characters. Audiences often think of them as being young forever. However, Raven-Symoné's fans were already used to seeing her mature on television. They have seen her grow from a chubby-cheeked young child star to a beautiful and self-assured young lady.

Raven-Symoné has enjoyed a successful career so far, and as she enters adulthood she is not about to slow down. Instead, she is ready to enter a new phase of her career. She has said that she would only like to take on projects that she can believe in, and does not want to do anything that would tarnish her good reputation among her young fans. She wants to continue providing entertainment that families can enjoy.

Forging ahead in different roles is nothing new. Raven-Symoné has been auditioning since she was a baby. She is used to taking on new roles, and trying new things. Along the way, she has developed a strong sense of who she is and what she wants to do with her life. Because of this, those who know Raven-Symoné believe that she will be able to succeed at whatever she tries. Debra Martin Chase, who was an executive producer on several of Raven-Symoné's movies, told *Ebony* magazine in 2007:

> **I think Raven has a very old soul and, in many respects, she is far beyond her years in terms of insight and judgment and the way she views the world. The challenge for her at this point, as it is for all young performers, is to transition her artistry into adulthood and both bring her young fan base along with her and build an older fan base.**

Good-Bye to Raven

When *That's So Raven* first began airing, Raven-Symoné was 17 years old. By the time she reached her early 20s, she was ready to move on to the next challenge. The final episodes of *That's So Raven* were filmed in 2006, with the last one airing on November 10, 2007.

Reruns of the show continued to be part of the Disney Channel lineup, and the show's episodes were also sold on DVD. The program remained popular with kids, and Raven-Symoné remained popular also. In 2008, she was again nominated for a Kids' Choice Award, as favorite television actress.

It was not easy for her to say good-bye to her television series, but she knew she had to move on and try new things. A year after the show ended she said:

> **CROSS-CURRENTS**
> The Kids' Choice Awards have been presented for more than 20 years. For some background, see "The Kids' Choice Awards." Go to page 54.

> **I miss the camaraderie between everybody. Even though we still talk, I miss seeing my [TV] family's faces everyday. We've all gone our own ways. But at the same time, we're all growing, and I think that's good.**

Taking a Road Trip

After the show ended, Raven-Symoné's first project after *Raven* was a movie that took advantage of her knack for comedy. In *College Road*

Beyond Raven

Raven-Symoné made a guest appearance on one episode of *Cory in the House*, a Disney Channel spinoff of *That's So Raven*. In the episode, Raven Baxter has to tackle the president to keep one of her wacky visions from coming true. Here, she is pictured with former *That's So Raven* costar Kyle Massey, the star of the new program.

Trip, she played a high school student who plans to check out colleges with some of her friends. Her father (played by comedian Martin Lawrence) has no intention of letting her do this by herself, however. He tags along on the trip and manages to get in her way at every turn. To make things interesting, a pig also joins them on the trip.

The movie was released in theaters in 2008 and had a G rating. It was a family friendly, funny movie. The film was designed to be entertainment that kids, teens, and parents could all enjoy and laugh at, without worrying about having to endure bad language or inappropriate scenes.

RAVEN-SYMONÉ

In the 2008 film *College Road Trip*, Raven-Symoné starred as a high-school student who is looking for the right college. Although it did not receive great reviews, the film was a hit. *College Road Trip* also starred another Disney Channel star, Brenda Song, as Raven's friend, and comedian Martin Lawrence as Raven's father.

Beyond Raven

This was the type of movie Raven-Symoné was excited about doing. It took advantage of her comic ability and her wholesome image. It appealed to her young fans, but also was a film that teens could identify with. The film was a modest hit, earning more than $45 million at the box office.

Raven-Symoné even recorded a song used in the movie, a remake of the early 1980s hit "Double Dutch Bus." The catchy song was also included on her fourth studio album, titled *Raven-Symoné*. To promote the new album, Raven-Symoné went on a "Pajama Party Tour," appearing at stadiums in more than 50 cities. Kids were encouraged to wear their pajamas to her performances.

On the Web

Movies, television, and music are not the only places Raven-Symoné has made her mark. After she was finished making her television series, she turned to the Internet to reach out to her fans.

The idea came to her one night while she was eating dinner. She wanted to create a Web site that would offer recipes, crafts, and quick tips for cleaning and clothing repairs. Not wanting to forget her brainstorm, she wrote her thoughts down on a napkin and brought the idea to her talent agent. Her advisors agreed that this Web site could be a great addition to her career. Raven-Symoné loves to cook and is a natural in front of the camera. A how-to Web site would allow her to combine her interest in cooking with her talent as an actress.

The Web site, called "Raven-Symoné Presents" (http://www.ravensymonepresents.com) was up and running by 2008. The site features the star talking to her fans. Through videos on the site, she demonstrates how to make a variety of sandwiches and create craft items such as a cloth journal cover and invitations. She also gives everyday advice, showing viewers how to fix a stuck zipper using olive oil and a Q-tip. She presents the information with enthusiasm and humor.

Raven-Symoné's Web site is not only a way for her to share information about crafts and recipes, it is also a savvy business venture. The huge telephone company AT&T sponsors the site, seeing it as an opportunity to promote its wireless products to teens. AT&T ring tones, phone features, and videos can be downloaded from Raven-Symoné's Web site.

RAVEN-SYMONÉ

➤ BEING HERSELF ➤

On the Web site, Raven-Symoné talks to her fans about everything from making a fuzzy pencil to deciding on which earrings to wear. She is not pretentious, and even asks viewers to bear with her if she is not wearing makeup. As she had done throughout her career, Raven-Symoné continues to be entertaining while being a positive role model for her fans.

Raven-Symoné does not go out of her way to draw attention to herself when she is not working, but one of the things she enjoys about being a star is the power it gives her to help others. Raven-Symoné loves helping kids and works with charities to support them. She was active in the March of Dimes, which is dedicated to improving the health of babies, and the Inner City Games, which aims to give inner-city children an opportunity to participate in sports and educational programs. She has also been very active with the Make-A-Wish Foundation, which attempts to enrich the lives of children with life-threatening illnesses by granting their wishes. In 2006, Raven-Symoné was rewarded for her charity work when she became the first person to receive the Disney VoluntEAR "Show Your Character" award. She was chosen for the award by Disney executives because of her work in the community.

CROSS-CURRENTS
Raven-Symoné has been involved with several charities. To learn more about one organization that she supports, read "The Make-A-Wish Foundation." Go to page 55.

The young actress does not help others for recognition, however. She does it because she wants to do what she can to help kids. The Inner City Games offers programs that help kids build self-esteem and confidence, and Raven likes how programs such as this give kids a safe place to learn. She is happy to help out in schools and do what she can to keep kids off the streets. She tries to help kids broaden their horizons and learn to work together. She sees this as a way she can make a difference:

> "I love doing things that help kids because—I know it sounds corny but it's true—kids are the future and will one day run the country, so we need to prepare children well so they can run the country with open minds and good hearts."

Beyond Raven

On the *Rachael Ray Show*, Raven showed how to make one of her two favorite meals, baked ziti. (The other is gumbo, a stew that is popular in the South.) She told *Time for Kids*, "Everyone who comes to my house always says, 'We're coming over! Can you cook the ziti or the gumbo?' And I'm like, 'Guys! (Sigh) OK.'"

≫ LOOKING AHEAD ≪

Raven-Symoné is happy to help out at charity events and offer tips on her Web site, but she gives few glimpses into her personal life beyond her interests in cooking and crafts. She prefers to keep to herself and stays quiet about her personal relationships. She does not hide from the public, and attends star-studded events, such as

RAVEN-SYMONÉ

the annual Essence Black Women in Hollywood luncheon. However, in interviews she prefers to talk about her career rather than her life at home.

Raven-Symoné has grown up in the public eye but always manages to keep her personal life private. She is very professional in

Raven-Symoné enjoys her success. "I'm happy and definitely focused, although in this industry you go through your ups-and-downs just because not everything is going to go your way," she told one interviewer. "Everybody has their days, but overall, yeah, I'm very happy with the way my life is going. And I'm healthy, and that should always make you happy."

her attitude toward her career, and prefers to be planning her next career move rather than thinking about going to clubs or parties.

Raven-Symoné enjoys what she does. She loves providing entertainment for people, whether it is through her acting or on her Web site. She envisions her Web site eventually leading to other things, perhaps a television show that focuses on home improvement, decorating, and crafts. Raven-Symoné sees herself as a type of Oprah Winfrey or Martha Stewart. She hopes to again have her own television show, but this time instead of playing a character, she will be herself. True to her style, she will be there to offer helpful tips and information.

Her plans do not stop there, however. In addition to a television show, she thinks about offering books and a line of home decorating items as well. She is not afraid to think big. Like the character she was best known for, Raven-Symoné is always looking to the future. She says:

> **"My goals are to have a TV show, to have licensing material, books . . . anything to decorate your house with, whether it's furniture, a craft book, ways to get your mind flowing. I have a five year, a ten year and a thirty year plan."**

With her numerous career successes to date, it is clear that Raven-Symoné is no ordinary celebrity. Surely the best is ahead for this intelligent and talented young performer.

CROSS-CURRENTS

Bill Cosby

The man who gave Raven-Symoné her start in television is a seasoned performer who cares about people. Bill Cosby has entertained audiences for five decades by telling funny stories that give insights into people's attitudes. He has achieved fame both for his stand-up comedy act and as the creator of several warm-hearted and educational television shows. He also encourages people to value education and take responsibility for their actions.

Cosby got his start during the 1960s, traveling across the nation doing stand-up comedy routines. He had a storytelling style that captured the audience's attention and made them smile. He appeared on *The Johnny Carson Show* and won five Grammy Awards for his comedy albums.

In 1965 the comedian made history when he was hired to star on the NBC television series *I Spy*. He became the first African American to receive a starring role in a dramatic television series. The show, which also starred Robert Culp, ran for four seasons and was very popular. Cosby won three Emmy Awards for his acting.

In the early 1970s, Cosby helped create an educational Saturday morning cartoon, *Fat Albert and the Cosby Kids*. The show was very popular and continued to be broadcast until the late 1980s. Cosby also

Bill Cosby was already one of America's most respected entertainers when he gave Raven-Symoné her start on television in 1989. Cosby gained fame in the 1960s as a stand-up comedian before moving to television. In addition to his groundbreaking Cosby Show, Bill Cosby worked on several educational TV programs for young people.

CROSS-CURRENTS

starred in the movie *Uptown Saturday Night*. But it was his role on a television show in the 1980s that sealed his fame.

In 1984 *The Cosby Show* was aired on NBC, featuring Cosby as Bill Huxtable. The episodes revolved around Cosby, who played a doctor, and his upper-middle-class family. Viewers of all races could identify with the Huxtables and the problems and humor they shared. *The Cosby Show* was the most popular sitcom on television during the 1980s, and won numerous Emmy and Golden Globe awards.

Cosby was also an author and created several other television shows after *The Cosby Show* ended. His shows include the animated series *Little Bill* and *Kids Say the Darndest Things* for the Nickelodeon channel. He continues to perform his stand-up comedy act as well.

Cosby is also known for being a good role model and creating a positive image for African Americans. He believes in education and taking responsibility. He wants people to learn positive parenting skills. He sees these as a way to help the lower-income communities in America. He has made free appearances across the United States to help people find solutions to improve the quality of their lives. His activism has earned him the Presidential Medal of Freedom and other honors. (Go back to page 5.) ◀◀

The NAACP Image Awards

The NAACP Image Awards are given each year to recognize the accomplishments of people of color in the entertainment industry. The awards were established in 1967 to honor outstanding black film and television actors and actresses, musicians, and writers.

Awards are given in numerous categories: five for motion pictures, 20 for television, nine for music, and three for literature. A Chairman's Award and President's Award are also given, and each year deserving entertainers are inducted into the NAACP Image Awards Hall of Fame. Hall of Fame members include Stevie Wonder, Ray Charles, and Bill Cosby.

The National Association for the Advancement of Colored People (NAACP), an influential civil rights organization that was founded in 1909, sponsors the Image Awards. The NAACP strives to make sure that the concerns of African Americans are heard. It has addressed issues in the entertainment industry since movies were in their infancy. In 1915, for example, the NAACP criticized the way African Americans were portrayed in the movie *Birth of a Nation*. The NAACP continues to encourage diversity in all parts of the entertainment industry.

Raven-Symoné has been honored with the NAACP Image Award for Outstanding Performance in a Youth/Children's Series or Special five times. She received the award each year from 2004 through 2008 for her work on *That's So Raven*. (Go back to page 8.) ◀◀

CROSS-CURRENTS

The Cosby Show

The Cosby Show, which gave Raven-Symoné her start as a television actress, began airing in 1984. The program about the Huxtable family revived the situation comedy, or sitcom, style of show. Each week viewers could tune in to see Dr. Heathcliff Huxtable (Bill Cosby), his wife Claire (Phylicia Rashad), and their five children (Sabrina LeBeauf as Sondra, Lisa Bonet as Denise, Malcolm-Jamal Warner as Theo, Tempestt Bledsoe as Vanessa, and Keisha-Knight Pulliam as Rudy) gently and humorously dealing with a different family crisis. The extremely popular show aired for eight consecutive seasons, and between 1985 and 1990 it was the No. 1 show on television.

The show marked an important moment in television as it featured a middle-class African-American family dealing with everyday problems. It promoted education, respect, and self-confidence. The Huxtables dealt with problems, from the death of a pet to birthday surprises, that all families could relate to, regardless of race. The show's last original episode aired in 1992. It remains popular in reruns on Nickelodeon and other channels.

Raven-Symoné played Olivia Kendall, the daughter of Denise's husband. She joined the cast in the show's sixth season (1989–90) and quickly became a fan favorite.

(Go back to page 12.) ◀◀

Julie Andrews

One of the movie stars Raven-Symoné admired while she was growing up was Julie Andrews. This talented actress and singer is known for her impressive voice range and work in such hit musicals as *Mary Poppins* and *The Sound of Music*. Andrews is also known to younger fans for her work as an author and in the *Princess Diaries* movies.

Andrews was born in 1935 in England. She began her career in vaudeville and at age 18 got her first role in a Broadway musical, *The Boy Friend*. Her work on the stage continued with the lead roles in *My Fair Lady* and *Camelot*. She was passed over for the lead in the movie version of *My Fair Lady* but her movie career took off in 1964 when she won the role of the magical governess Mary Poppins in the hit Disney film of the same name. The role earned her an Academy Award. She was nominated for a second Academy Award for her role as Maria von Trapp in *The Sound of Music* (1965).

Andrews began writing children's books during the 1970s. Under the name Julie Edwards, she wrote *Mandy*, after she lost a bet with her stepdaughter. Her other books include *The Last of the Really Great Whangdoodles* and stories about a kitten named Little Bo, including *Little Bo: The Story of Bonnie Boadicea*. She has also collaborated with her daughter, Emma Walton Hamilton, on a series of

CROSS-CURRENTS

books about a dump truck. The series includes *Dumpy the Dumptruck* and *Dumpy at School*.

Andrews returned to Broadway in the late 1990s with the musical *Victor/Victoria*. However, in 1997 she had an operation to remove a polyp from her vocal cords. Her voice was much weaker after the operation. Her career on Broadway ended, but she continued to make movies.

In 2001, Andrews took on the role of Queen Clarisse Renaldi in the movie *The Princess Diaries*. She met Raven-Symoné when she played the character again in the 2004 Disney movie *The Princess Diaries 2: Royal Engagement*. She also played a queen in the second and third *Shrek* movies, voicing Queen Lillian in the animated films.

Andrews is married to film producer Blake Edwards and has three daughters and two stepchildren. She has received Oscar, Emmy, and Tony awards, for work in movies, on television, and on the stage. In 2000 she received the title "dame" from Queen Elizabeth II.

(Go back to page 27.) ◄◄

This famous scene featuring Julie Andrews appears at the beginning of The Sound of Music. *Andrews, one of the 20th century's most recognizable actresses, has won many awards for her work. Raven-Symoné has said that Julie Andrews is one of her role models, and was thrilled to work with Andrews on the 2004 film* Princess Diaries 2: Royal Engagement.

CROSS-CURRENTS

Raven's Secret

Raven's knack for comedy earned her loyal fans. The secret to her success was her willingness to take risks with her character. She did not worry about people laughing at her—that was what she hoped to accomplish. Although *That's So Raven* was a comedy, Raven approached her work seriously. She played a wacky character who prompted laughs from the audience, but it took a great deal of hard work to achieve that result.

In 2006, Gary Marsh, the Disney Channel Worldwide president of entertainment, told *The Hollywood Reporter* why he thought Raven was so popular with viewers:

"Raven's gift is that she is not just funny—which she is, hysterically funny—but the reason that she's a star is that she's fearless and creates laughs at her own expense. She will try anything to add more comedy to a gag, like a pratfall, or change her delivery 180 degrees. The true crucible for her is if she gets a laugh out of the audience. If she doesn't she'll demand another take."

Raven was proud of the show. Like *Cosby*, it presented a middle-class African American family dealing with ordinary problems. Although Raven always got into sticky situations, she always tried to do what was best.

(Go back to page 27.)

Raven-Symoné as Lucille Ball in this image from the season four episode of That's So Raven, *entitled "Soup to Nuts." Lucille Ball (1911–1989) was an iconic American comedienne who appeared on television and in films from the 1930s to the 1970s.*

CROSS-CURRENTS 53

Who's Who in *The Cheetah Girls*

The Disney Channel's popular *Cheetah Girls* movies are based on a book series by Deborah Gregory. They feature four girls from different backgrounds who come together to form a pop group and have their eyes on stardom. The cast of the movies include (as the four Cheetahs):

Chanel, played by Adrienne Bailon. In the original movie, Chanel is unsure of her mother's relationship with her boyfriend. She is hurt when her mother forgets their shopping date.

Aquanetta, played by Kiely Williams. In *The Cheetah Girls 2*, she finds that she loves fashion.

Dorinda, played by Sabrina Bryan. Dorinda is a foster child who is embarrassed to be living in a small apartment with nine other foster children. She has a talent for dancing, and must choose between a part with a dance troupe and performing with the Cheetah Girls.

Galleria, played by Raven-Symoné. As the leader of the Cheetah Girls, she's driven to help them succeed. However, she has a hard time taking the other girls' views into account. In *The Cheetah Girls*, she finds that the group members are her true friends when they help save her dog after it falls into a manhole.

Kiely Williams, Sabrina Bryan, Adrienne Bailon, and Raven-Symoné pose for a photo promoting their 2006 film The Cheetah Girls 2. *On the soundtrack for the second film in the series, Raven sang three songs by herself. She also joined the other three Cheetahs for several numbers. Both of the* Cheetah Girls *films were very successful for Disney.*

(Go back to page 31.) ⏪

CROSS-CURRENTS

The Kids' Choice Awards

Raven-Symoné has been nominated for a Kids' Choice Award as Best Television Actress four times. The awards are an annual tribute to the shows, movies, actors, and actresses that kids like best. Kids get a chance to choose the winners by voting online, over the phone, or through sponsors.

The shows at which the Kids' Choice Awards are presented, which are held every spring, are far from boring. The award winners, host, and presenters never know when they are going to get hit with slime. The green, gooey slime pours out at surprising times during each show. Stars from Will Smith to Tom Cruise and Jack Black have all been covered in slime.

The show's winners are also announced in unusual ways. The winner's name might be carried in by an animal or dropped from the ceiling on a banner.

The show got its start in 1986. Nickelodeon asked kids for their opinion in the Big Ballot poll. The poll turned into the Kids' Choice Awards, which debuted in 1987. In 1988, the show began adding performances to its lineup. The first performers on the Kids' Choice Awards show were The New Kids on the Block.

In 1990, award winners began being honored with trophies in the shape of a blimp. Winners that year included Michael Jordan, Michael J. Fox, and *The Cosby Show*. The hosts that year were Dave Coulier of *Full House*, along with David Faustino of *Married With Children* and Candace Cameron of *Full House*. Candace's brother Kirk also won an award, for Favorite TV Actor.

In 1991, the show began giving a Hall of Fame award. The first winner of this award was Paula Abdul. In 1996, she presented the Hall of Fame award to Tim Allen. In 2001, the Hall of Fame Award was replaced with the Wannabe Award, which is given to the best celebrity role model. Winners of this award include Ben Stiller in 2007 and Cameron Diaz in 2008.

The show has also given awards for many things adults would find repulsive, such as best burp. Some celebrities have not been shy about competing for this award. Cameron Diaz won the first Best Burp award in 2001. Justin Timberlake won in 2003.

The show attracted kids' favorite stars as hosts and presenters. Stars such as Brad Pitt, Will Smith, Shaquille O'Neal, Robert DeNiro, and Madonna have appeared on the show. Hosts have included Rosie O'Donnell, Jack Black, Ben Stiller, Cameron Diaz, and Mike Myers. (Go back to page 40.)

CROSS-CURRENTS

The Make-A-Wish Foundation

Raven-Symoné is an avid supporter of the Make-A-Wish Foundation. The organization helps children with life-threatening illnesses by giving them hope and joy through the wishes it grants for them. Raven-Symoné believed in the organization's mission so much that she tried to grant every request she received. She fulfilled dozens of wishes for the organization.

The organization was founded in 1980. The first wish was granted to a seven-year-old boy with leukemia who dreamed of being a police officer. From there, the organization grew to one that helps children all over the world. Children between the ages of two-and-a-half and 18 can have their wishes granted by the Make-A-Wish Foundation. The children must have been diagnosed with a medical condition that is life-threatening. A wish team helps the children find their true wish and works to make that wish come true.

Most children ask to go somewhere, meet someone, take on a profession for a day, or receive a special gift. Some children wish to meet celebrities or sports figures. Others want to ride a horse, watch a volcano erupt, or swim with dolphins. Many children want to visit theme parks—almost half of the wishes granted involve Disney.

Raven-Symoné became involved with Make-A-Wish when she was about 15 years old. She went with kids whose wishes were granted to events on Disney Cruise ships and invited kids to visit the set of her show and see the launch of her fragrance. For kids who were too sick to travel, she taped a personal message for them. When Disney held a special event in 2005 to raise money for the Make-A-Wish Foundation, a 12-year-old named Ashley from Mississippi had her wish granted by Raven-Symoné. She wanted to see what it was like to be a star and attend a red carpet event with Raven-Symoné. She got to ride in a limousine to an event on a Disney Cruise ship, walk the red carpet with Raven-Symoné, and sign autographs with the star.

Raven-Symoné explained why she wanted to be involved with the Make-A-Wish Foundation in an interview with *Seventeen Magazine*:

> **"These kids talk about their illnesses every day of their lives—this is one day where it's about them and not the disease. To know that other people want you to survive and be a part of their lives is a great feeling for them. The more support a child can feel, the better."**

(Go back to page 44.) ⏪

CHRONOLOGY

1985   Raven-Symoné Pearman is born on December 10.

1987   She begins modeling at 16 months old.

1989   An audition for Bill Cosby's movie *Ghost Dad* leads to Raven-Symoné's role as Olivia on *The Cosby Show*.

1993   The single "That's What Little Girls Are Made Of" marks the beginning of Raven-Symoné's career as a professional singer.

         She is cast as Nicole in *Hangin' with Mr. Cooper*.

1994   Raven-Symoné makes her movie debut in *The Little Rascals*.

1998   She plays opposite Eddie Murphy in the comedy *Dr. Dolittle*, in the role of his daughter.

1999   Her album *Undeniable* is released.

         She goes on tour and opens for the pop band 'N Sync.

2002   Raven-Symoné begins voicing Monique on the animated series *Kim Possible*.

2003   She gets her own television show on the Disney Channel, *That's So Raven*.

         She is featured in the television movie *The Cheetah Girls*.

2004   She releases the album *This Is My Time*.

2006   *The Cheetah Girls 2* is released, along with a soundtrack for the movie.

         Raven-Symoné releases a solo album, *From Then Until*.

2008   Raven-Symoné stars in the movie *College Road Trip* with Martin Lawrence.

         She hosts a Web site filled with recipes, crafts, and tips.

ACCOMPLISHMENTS & AWARDS

Filmography
- **1994** *The Little Rascals*
- **1998** *Dr. Dolittle*
- **2001** *Dr. Dolittle 2*
  Fat Albert
- **2004** *The Princess Diaries 2: Royal Engagement*
- **2006** *Everyone's Hero*
- **2008** *College Road Trip*

Awards and Award Nominations
- **1990** Nominated, Young Artist Award, Outstanding Performance by a Young Actress Under Nine (*The Cosby Show*)
- **1991** Young Artist Award, Exceptional Performance by a Young Actress Under Nine (*The Cosby Show*)
- **1993** Nominated, Young Artist Award, Outstanding Actress Under Ten in a Television Series (*The Cosby Show*)
- **1994** Nominated, Young Artist Award, Best Youth Comedienne (*Hangin' with Mr. Cooper*)
- **1996** Nominated, NAACP Image Award, Outstanding Youth Actor/Actress (*Hangin' with Mr. Cooper*)
- **1999** Nominated, Young Star Award, Best Performance by a Young Actress in a Mini-series/Made for TV Film (*Zenon: Girl of the 21st Century*)
- **2002** Nominated, NAACP Image Award, Outstanding Youth Actor/Actress (*Dr. Dolittle 2*)

  Nominated, Kids' Choice Award, Favorite Female Movie Star (*Dr. Dolittle 2*)
- **2004** NAACP Image Award, Outstanding Performance in a Youth/Children's Program (*That's So Raven*)

  Kids' Choice Award, Favorite Television Actress (*That's So Raven*)

  Nominated, BET Comedy Award, Outstanding Lead Actress in a Comedy Series (*That's So Raven*)

  Nominated, Black Reel Award, Television: Best Actress (*The Cheetah Girls*)

  Nominated, Teen Choice Awards, Choice TV Actress: Comedy (*That's So Raven*)

  Nominated, Young Artist Award, Best Performance in a TV Series (Comedy or Drama) - Leading Young Actress (*That's So Raven*)

ACCOMPLISHMENTS & AWARDS

2005   NAACP Image Award, Outstanding Performance in a Youth/Children's Program (*That's So Raven*)

Kids' Choice Award, Favorite Television Actress (*That's So Raven*)

Young Artist Award, Outstanding Young Performers in a TV Series (with Orlando Brown, Kyle Massey, and Anneliese van der Pol for *That's So Raven*)

Nominated, BET Comedy Award, Best Performance in an Animated Theatrical Film (*Kim Possible: So the Drama*)

Nominated, BET Comedy Award, Outstanding Lead Actress in a Comedy Series (*That's So Raven*)

Nominated, Teen Choice Awards, Choice TV Actress: Comedy (*That's So Raven*)

2006   NAACP Image Award, Outstanding Performance in a Youth/Children's Program (*That's So Raven*)

Nominated, Kids' Choice Award, Favorite Television Actress (*That's So Raven*)

Nominated, Teen Choice Awards, Choice TV Actress: Comedy (*That's So Raven*)

2007   NAACP Image Award, Outstanding Performance in a Youth/Children's Program (*That's So Raven*)

NAMIC North Star Award

Nominated, NAACP Image Award, Outstanding Actress in a Comedy Series (*That's So Raven*)

Nominated, Kids' Choice Award, Favorite Television Actress (*That's So Raven*)

2008   Nominated, NAACP Image Award, Outstanding Performance in a Youth/Children's Program (*That's So Raven*)

Nominated, NAMIC Vision Award, Best Performance—Comedy (*That's So Raven*)

FURTHER READING & INTERNET RESOURCES

Books
Leavitt, Amie Jane, *Raven-Symoné*, Hockessin, Delaware: Mitchell Lane Publishers, 2008.

Magazines
Abbott, Denise. "Rave on!" *The Hollywood Reporter–International Edition*. August 1, 2006, p. S2.

Bryson, Jodi. "Raven Is So Like That!" *Girls' Life*. October/November 2004, p. 28.

Cole, Harriette. "Raven Symoné: From Cosby Kid to the Disney Dynasty, Raven-Symoné Speaks Candidly About Growing up on and off Screen." *Ebony*, February 21, 2007.

Goodman, Brenda. "That's So Refreshing." *Atlanta*, February 2006, p. 22.

Us Magazine, "Raven-Symoné: How I Stay Out of Trouble," January 31, 2008, www.usmagazine.com/raven_symone_how_i_stay_out_of_trouble.

Web Sites

www.ravensymonepresents.com
On Raven-Symoné's Web site, she offers tips on everything from cleaning to cooking. She also features craft ideas and describes how to make them.

www.disneychannel.com
Find information on *That's So Raven*, *The Cheetah Girls*, and other Disney Channel shows and stars by searching on this site.

www.imdb.com
The Internet Movie Database contains listings of stars' movies.

www.people.com
The Web site for *People* magazine has the latest information on the activities of famous people.

www.tv.com
Find information on television shows on this site. Search for *That's So Raven* or *The Cosby Show* to learn about each program and see an episode listing.

Publisher's note:
The Web sites mentioned in this book were active at the time of publication. The publisher is not responsible for Web sites that have changed their addresses or discontinued operation since the date of publication. The publisher will review and update the Web site addresses each time the book is reprinted.

GLOSSARY

Animated film—A show made from a series of drawings; a cartoon.

Audition—To try out for a role in a television show or movie.

Contract—A legal agreement.

Costars—The actors and actresses who perform together in a show.

Episode—One show in a series.

Mug—To make faces.

Music video—A recorded performance of a song or a series of images shown with a song released by a performer.

Pratfall—an embarrassing fall, often done deliberately to be funny.

Producer—A person who oversees or provides money for a television show, movie, or play.

Reruns—A movie or television show that is shown again.

Role—A part in a show played by an actress or actor.

Sequel—A movie, television show, or book that continues a story from a previous work and uses the same characters.

Series—A set of television shows that appear regularly.

Sitcom—A situation comedy. A television comedy series that features the same, or almost the same, cast of characters and setting in each episode.

Soundtrack—The music from a television show or movie that is released on a CD.

Typecast—To often cast an actress or actor in similar roles.

NOTES

p. 6 "A very talented young actress . . ." Denise Abbott, "Rave on!" *The Hollywood Reporter*, August 1, 2006, p. S2.

p. 9 "I'm focusing on girl power . . ." Abbott, "Rave on!," p. S2.

p. 9 "Being beautiful is not . . ." Jodi Bryson, "Raven Is So Like That," *Girl's Life* (October/November 2004), p. 48.

p. 15 "Working with her and seeing . . ." Allison Samuels, "Why Not Raven?" *Newsweek* (August 1, 2005), p. 50.

p. 15 "I've gotten rejected so many . . ." PBSKids.org, "It's My Life," http://pbskids.org/itsmylife/celebs/interviews/raven2.html.

p. 15 "I get there and there'd be . . ." PBSKids.org, "It's My Life," http://pbskids.org/itsmylife/celebs/interviews/raven.html.

p. 17 "People always ask me . . ." Fern Gillespie, "Raven-Symoné plays Dr. Dolittle's Daughter," *New York Amsterdam News* (July 9, 1998), p. 21.

p. 20 "It showed me that . . ." PBSKids.org, "It's My Life."

p. 22 "She has that intangible . . ." Heather Keets Wright, "Raven Wins Raves," *Essence* (October 2003), p. 148.

p. 22 "I love the Cheetah girls . . ." "Raven-Symoné," *Scholastic Action* (November 3, 2003), p. 15.

p. 23 "The cast is so diverse . . ." *Jet* (August 21, 2006), p. 48.

p. 25 "I want people to hear . . ." Bryson, "Raven Is So Like That," p. 48.

p. 26 "Raven Baxter is so . . ." PBSkids.org, "It's My Life."

p. 27 "I got to sing with . . ." Bryson, "Raven Is So Like That," p. 48.

p. 27 "I met Janet Jackson . . ." Bryson, "Raven Is So Like That," p. 48.

p. 30 "She's so on the mark . . ." Michelle Grabicki, "The Raven's Song," *The Hollywood Reporter*, August 1, 2006, p. S8.

p. 32 "By the end I . . ." Samuels, "Why Not Raven?," p. 50.

p. 32 "I'm not going to change . . ." Brenda Goodman, "That's so refreshing," *Atlanta* (February 2006), p. 22.

p. 35 "We see someone who is . . ." Samuels, "Why Not Raven?," p. 50.

p. 36 "I'm a homebody . . ." "Raven-Symoné: How I Stay Out of Trouble," *US Magazine* (January 31, 2008). http://www.usmagazine.com/raven_symone_how_i_stay_out_of_trouble

p. 37 "If you find me on . . ." PBSKids.org, "It's My Life."

p. 37 "My fans all know . . ." Samuels, "Why Not Raven," p. 50.

p. 40 "I think Raven has . . ." Harriette Cole, "Raven-Symoné: from Cosby Kid to the Disney Dynasty," *Ebony* (March 2007), p. 58.

p. 40 "I miss the camaraderie . . ." Vickie An, "Q&A with Raven-Symoné," *Post-Bulletin.com* (March 18, 2008). www.postbulletin.com/newsmanager/templates/localnews_story.asp?a=333550&z=19

NOTES

p. 44 "I love doing things . . ." PBSKids.org, "It's My Life."

p. 45 "Everyone who comes . . ." Vicky An, "Ten Questions for Raven-Symoné," *Time for Kids* (March 6, 2008). http://www.timeforkids.com/TFK/kids/news/story/0,28277,1720467,00.html

p. 46 "I'm happy and definitely focused . . ." Kam Williams, "Interview with Raven-Symoné," *News Blaze* (March 3, 2008). http://newsblaze.com/story/20080303140404tsop.nb/topstory.html

p. 47 "My goals are to have . . ." "Raven-Symoné: How I Stay Out of Trouble," *US Magazine* (January 31, 2008). http://www.usmagazine.com/raven_symone_how_i_stay_out_of_trouble.

p. 52 "Raven's gift is that . . ." *Hollywood Reporter*, "100 Episodes: Now That's SO Raven!," August 1, 2006, p. S11.

p. 54 ""These kids talk about . . ." "Raven-Symoné's Mission: Make Dreams Come True," *Seventeen Magazine* (March 2008), p. 136.

INDEX

Absolutely Psychic. See *That's So Raven*
Andrews, Julie, 25, 27, 50–51

Bailon, Adrienne, 22, **23**, 53
Brown, Orlando, 19, **21**
Bryan, Sabrina, 22, **23**, 53

charity work, 6, 8–9, 17, 44–45, 55
Chase, Debra Martin, 22, 40
The Cheetah Girls, 22–24, 53
The Cheetah Girls 2, 30–31, 53
College Road Trip, 40–43
Cory in the House, **41**
Cosby, Bill, 5, 12, 32, 48–50
The Cosby Show, 5, **10**, 12, **13**, **14**, 48–50
Curry, Mark, 14

Dr. Dolittle, 15, 17

Ella Enchanted, 27

For One Night, 32–33
The Fresh Prince of Bel-Air, 13–14
From Then Until (album), 34

Gregory, Deborah, 53

Hangin' with Mr. Cooper, 6, 14–15
Happily Ever After, 17
Hathaway, Anne, 25

Jackson, Janet, 27

Kemiah, T'Keyah Crystal, 19, **21**
Kids' Choice Awards, 54
Kim Possible, 20, 22, 31–32

Lawrence, Martin, 41, **42**

Make-A-Wish Foundation, 8, 44, 55
Marsh, Gary, 52
Mary Poppins, 27, 50
Massey, Kyle, 19, **21**, **41**
McCrary, Gerica, **33**
Murphy, Eddie, 15
My Wife and Kids, 17

NAACP Image Awards, **4**, 5, 9, 49
Nash, Niecy, **8**
National Association for Multi-ethnicity in Communications (NAMIC), **8**
North Star Award, **8**

Pearman, Blaize (brother), 11
Pearman, Christopher (father), 11
Pearman, Lydia Gaulden (mother), 11
Pearman, Raven-Symoné Christina. See Raven-Symoné
The Princess Diaries 2, 25, 27, 51
The Proud Family, 17

Rachael Ray Show, **45**
Raven-Symoné
  awards won by, **4**, 5, **8**, 9, 12, 20, 44, 49, 54
  birth and childhood, 10–12
  business empire of, 6–7, 35
  and celebrity, 35–37, 45–47
  charity work, 6, 8–9, 17, 44–45, 55
  on *The Cosby Show,* 5–6, **10**, 12, **13**, 48–50
  on *Hangin' with Mr. Cooper,* 6, 14–15
  on *Kim Possible,* 20, 22, 31–32
  and modeling, 11
  and movies, 6, 14, 15, 17, 22–23, 25, 27, 30–33, 39–43, 53
  and name changes, 19, 29
  production company, **28**
  and school, 15–17
  and singing career, 12–13, 17, 24–25, 27, 30–31, 34–35, 43
  on *That's So Raven,* 5, 6, 9, 18–21, 28–30, 35, 40, 49, 52
  Web site of, **38**, 43–45, 47
Raven-Symoné (album), 43
"Raven-Symoné Presents" (Web site), **38**, 43–45, 47

Sheridan, Rondell, **8**, 19, **21**
Song, Brenda, **42**

That's So Productions, **28**
That's So Raven, 5, 6, 9, 18–21, 28–30, 35, 40, 49, 52
This Is My Time (album), 24–25, 27
Trippe, Ron, 6

Undeniable (album), 17, **34**

van der Poi, Anneliese, 19, **21**

Whiteside, Damon, 30
Williams, Kiely, 22, **23**, 53

Zenon: Girl of the 21st Century, 17

Numbers in **bold italics** refer to captions.

ABOUT THE AUTHOR

Terri Dougherty has written more than 60 books for children. She lives in Appleton, Wisconsin, with her husband, Denis, and their three children. She enjoys learning new things with every book she writes.

PICTURE CREDITS

page

- **1:** AdMedia Photos
- **4:** Frank Micelotta/Getty Images for NAACP
- **7:** EBONY/NMI
- **8:** NAMIC/NMI
- **10:** ASP Library
- **13:** NBC/NMI
- **14:** ABC/NMI
- **16:** ASP Library
- **18:** Disney Channel/PRMS
- **21:** Disney Channel/PRMS
- **23:** Walt Disney Pictures/NMI
- **24:** Vanity Fair/NMI
- **26:** Salon City/NMI
- **28:** Disney Channel/NMI
- **31:** Disney Channel/NMI
- **33:** Lifetime/NMI
- **34:** TMG/NMI
- **36:** Milk PEP/NMI
- **38:** AdMedia Photos
- **41:** Disney Channel/NMI
- **42:** Walt Disney Pictures/NMI
- **45:** CIC Photos
- **46:** Chad Buchanan/Getty Images
- **48:** NBC/NMI
- **51:** Twentieth Century Fox/NMI
- **52:** Disney Channel/PRMS
- **53:** Walt Disney Pictures/PRMS

Front cover: Disney Channel/PRMS